How to be a
WORRY
DETECTIVE

Becoming the boss of your brain and body!

Written by Hara Howard

This book is dedicated to my two amazing children.
who push me to face my worries every day

This book belongs to:

_____

Worry likes to be the boss of our minds and bodies.
Do you ever have a worry?

Worry can be confusing because it can be helpful, like when we detect real danger.

When worry tricks us, we can feel uneasy, nervous, frightened, or even angry. These emotions can seem out of our control.

The good news is, you can learn to be a worry detective! A worry detective has the power to change what they think, feel, and do. A worry detective takes control back from worry and can even change their brain so that they worry less. Do you want to become a worry detective?

Before you can become a worry detective, it is important to remember one thing: Your worry is not a part of you. It may trick you into thinking it is, but YOU are stronger than your worry and have what it takes to become the boss!

Your worry will make you feel strange and tell you all kinds of stories to try and stay in charge. But remember, YOU ARE THE BOSS!

Are you ready to learn the steps you can take to become a worry detective and become the boss of your own mind and body?

Great! Let's go!

Step 1: Recognize your worry

Our minds and bodies give us clues to find a worry. What does your worry say to you? How does it make your body feel?

Step 2: Name and picture your worry

Remember, you are NOT your worry even when it feels like worry has taken over. Naming your worry helps to separate it from the brave kid you can be! Picturing what your worry looks like will remind you that it is not a part of you.

Oh, that's just Wanda trying to be the boss of me again!

What will you name your worry? What does it look like?

Tip: It's very helpful to draw a picture of your worry!

Step 3: Face your worry.

Now that you've named your worry, it's time to teach the worry who is boss! Avoiding your worry will only give it more power. When you give worry power, you can miss out on really fun and exciting things!

Step 4: Change the story
This is where the magic happens!

Now that you've faced your worry, you have the power to change the stories your worry tells you. The coolest part? A worry detective can change their own brain! Each time you change the story, your brain gets stronger and the worry gets less powerful. Over time, the worry stops coming!

The stories your worry tells you are called unhelpful thoughts. Once you recognize these unhelpful thoughts, you have the power to replace them with a helpful thought.

Let's talk about five unhelpful thoughts your worry will tell you. Once you practice recognizing these unhelpful thoughts, you can replace the thought and outsmart your worry! The more you practice, the easier it is to recognize them. You can also keep this book nearby as a detective tool!

The first type of unhelpful thought your worry may tell you is called **all or nothing** thinking. All or nothing thinking can make us believe that things are either all good or all bad instead of recognizing the in-between. A good detective will recognize an all or nothing thought and replace it with a helpful fact.

The second type of unhelpful thought that worry will tell you is called labeling . Worry may try to label a situation or person with a name such as 'scary'. 'hard'. or 'mean' instead of looking at the facts. When you detect worry tricking you with a label. you can outsmart worry with a helpful fact instead.

LABELING

The third type of unhelpful thought that your worry uses to trick you is called fortune telling . Worry will pretend they can see the future by telling you what will happen. As a detective, you won't let worry's fortune telling trick you. You are becoming a pro at this, and will replace the unhelpful thought with a helpful fact.

If you go to the party you will be too afraid to talk to other kids and will have no one to play with

I have had fun at parties before, and even if you don't know everyone, you can be brave and meet someone new

FORTUNE TELLING

The fourth type of unhelpful thought that worry will use to trick you is called magnifying. The negative part of something will get bigger and the positive part will get smaller. As a detective, it's your job to make sure you point out the positive parts of a situation when worry keeps telling you the negative. Each time you do this, your brain gets stronger and worry will become scared!

The fifth type of unhelpful thought that worry will use is called should-ing. Worry will try to tell you that you 'should' or 'must' do something. Recognizing these unhelpful thoughts can give you a lot of power over worry. As a detective, you will be ready to combat worry and replace these 'should' or 'must' thoughts with helpful facts.

Now that you know what thoughts worry will use to trick you, you can practice replacing worry's thoughts with helpful ones. Practicing these steps will allow you to defeat worry and become the boss of your body and brain!

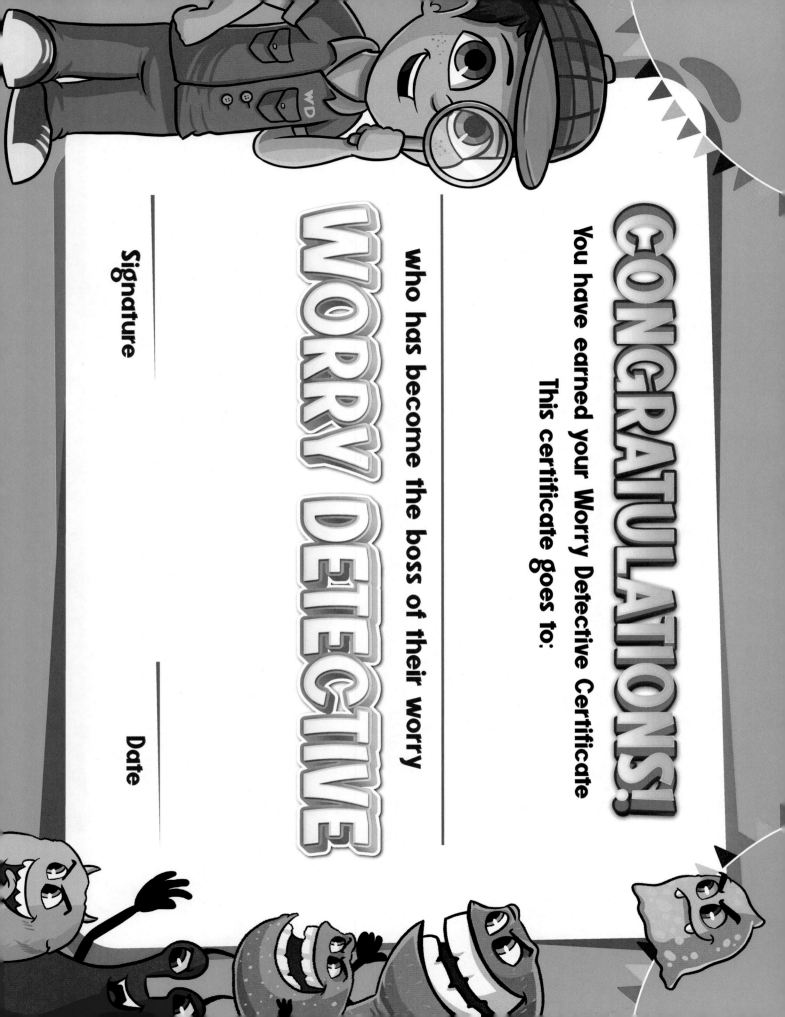

The more you practice, the better a detective you'll become! Ask an adult for help, and track/change some of your own unhelpful thoughts. Stand up to worry so that you can take control of your own life!

Unhelpful Thought	Type of Thought	Replacement Thought
If I'm not good at soccer my friends won't like me	All or nothing thinking	Everyone on the team tries their best and my friends and I have fun

Strategies for Parents to support anxious kids:

As a parent, it can be difficult to watch your child struggle. Here are some ideas to help support your worrier:

- Always remember that avoiding a situation will only increase the anxiety that surrounds it. The only way to get over something is to get through it.

- Model your own worries. Recognize when you are having a negative thought and normalize it. Kids need to know they are not alone.

- Role play! You be worry and have your child become the boss of you (then switch roles). Don't forget to use worry's name! Or, if you are feeling extra fun, dress up!

- Have fun with it and use humor! Remember, the key is to build a trusting relationship which allows kids to take risks.

- Keep a jar of positive thoughts at home and read them often (the more you do this, the more your brain will believe them).

- Gratitude! Use a gratitude journal, or talk about all of the things you are grateful for. This will also start to outweigh negative thinking and neuroplasticity will occur

- Find the balance of support and expectations. You can provide love and support while pushing them to face their fears.

Real Kids - Real Worries

Worry Spins
Tiba, age 6

Anxious Andre
Aaron, age 12

Worry Dog
Blair, age 11

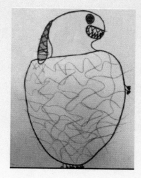

Scaredy
Vida, age 7

Fire-ena
Quinn, age 8.5

Deflate
Jaxson, age 6

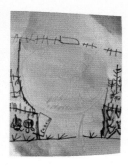

Eyeball
Fiona, age 8

Worry Monster
Harper, age 5.5

Worry Monster
Max, age 6

Anxious Emoji
Hailey, age 11

Red
Morgan, age 8

Sam Spider
Hayden, age 9

Worry Rob
Mackenzie, age 8

TAC Monster
Maya, age 7

Puking Petunia
Theo, age 8

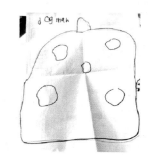

Dogman
Jaxson, age 7

Made in the USA
Columbia, SC
18 July 2023

20605831R00018